Other books about Ricky

Knight Ricky
Ricky
Ricky and Annie
Ricky and Mia the Chicken
Ricky and the Squirrel

First published in Belgium and Holland by Clavis Uitgeverij, Hasselt – Amsterdam, 2004
Copyright © 2004, Clavis Uitgeverij

English translation from the Dutch by Clavis Publishing Inc. New York
Copyright © 2011 for the English language edition: Clavis Publishing Inc. New York

Visit us on the web at www.clavisbooks.com – www.guidovangenechten.be

Ricky's Christmas Tree written and illustrated by Guido van Genechten
Original title: *Rikki wil een kerstboom*
Translated from the Dutch by Clavis Publishing
English language edition edited by Emma D. Dryden, drydenbks llc

ISBN 978-1-60537-106-1

This book was printed in May 2011 at Proost,
Everdongenlaan 23, B-2300 Turnhout, Belgium

First Edition
10 9 8 7 6 5 4 3 2 1

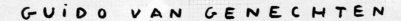

GUIDO VAN GENECHTEN

RICKY'S
CHRISTMAS TREE

Clavis

NEW YORK

It is almost Christmas, but Ricky's family doesn't have a
Christmas tree yet.
Dad and Mom have both been too busy to get one.
"I would really love to get a Christmas tree," Ricky says.

Dad sighs. "Not now, son, I've got too much work to do."
"We cannot have Christmas without a tree," Ricky insists. "Come on, Dad,
let's go and get one right now!" Ricky jumps up, grabs their scarves,
and stands by the open door.
"Alright, let's go," Dad says. "But let's make it quick."

"Look!" Ricky points. "I'd love an ice-carrot."
Dad pulls one from the edge of their roof.
"Come on, Ricky," he says, "we don't have all day, you know."

"Try my ice-carrot, Dad,
it tastes like a real popsicle!"
"No." Dad shakes his head.
"I'm too cold."

"Look!" Ricky calls out. "Cat tracks. Just look at
this, Dad, you can see where she ran!"
"Yes, yes," Dad mutters. "We don't have time for that now.
Hurry up and then we'll be back sooner."

the Christmas tree market Dad points to the very first Christmas tree he sees.
"his one here, please," he says to the vendor.

But Ricky sees a tree that he thinks is much nicer.
"No, that one over there," Ricky says. "I want that big one there!"
"Alright," Dad gives in with a shrug. "Let's go home with this big tree for my small boy."

Together they bind the Christmas tree to their sled.
"I'll pull the sled," Ricky says excitedly, grabbing the rope.
"Alright, but it might be too slow going."

Dad helps Ricky when they start up a long hill because
it is rather heavy, such a big Christmas tree on a sled.
"One, two, hop!" Ricky calls. "One, two, hop!"

Oops!
The rope breaks and Ricky and Dad fall
on their bottoms in the snow.
Head over heels they tumble down the hill,
all the way down … down … down.

Ricky is the first to scramble to his feet. He shrieks with laughter when he sees Dad sitting there, all covered in snow.
"You look like a funny snowman!"

Dad looks a little embarrassed, but then he starts laughing too.
"Here, take that!" he shouts, throwing a snowball.
Snowballs fly through the air.
Dad ducks away, but Ricky keeps throwing.
Yeah, that one hit the target!

For a long while they play together. Ricky wins
an exciting snow race and balances on top of a big
snowball. And then they perform in Ricky's Snow Circus!

Totally exhausted, they let themselves fall back into the snow.
"Snow is so much fun," Dad says. "I nearly forgot about that."
"I didn't," Ricky says with a smile.

They have a look at the snow-rabbit prints they've made in the snow.

"Yours is bigger than mine, Dad."

"You'll be as big and tall as I am when you're older," Dad says, "maybe even taller."

Yes, Ricky hopes he'll be even bigger and stronger!
He pushes the Christmas tree back onto the sled.
Dad re-ties the rope and the two of them pull the sled home.

"Oh, you've found the most perfect Christmas tree for us!" Mom exclaims.

I picked it," Ricky says proudly, "and I pulled the sled, and Dad was a funny
snowman and we played in the snow, didn't we, Dad?"
"Sounds like fun," Mom says and she gives her two men a big kiss on their
cold cheeks.

Together they decorate the tree. Ricky puts the star on top.
And when it's quite dark outside,
he switches on the twinkling tree lights.
"You know," Dad says, "when I was little, I always wanted a big tree like th
"Me, too," Mom says, "with big red balls and silver garlands,
and lights and a star, just like Ricky's tree."

"I still have a piece of ice-carrot in my pocket," Ricky says.
"Will you share it with me, Dad?"
"Of course, Ricky," says Dad.
"Merry Christmas."